The Unicorn Prince

Saviour Pirotta and Jane Ray

ORCHARD

High on a hill, where the moors ended and the forest began, stood a lonely castle. It had once been glorious but now the wind howled through its forgotten corridors and rain pelted in through its broken roof.

Only two people lived in the castle. A young woman called Annis and her grandmother.

The only warm, dry spot in this crumbling castle was in front of the great fireplace, and it was here that Annis and her grandmother slept – along with their chickens and their cow. It was a bit of a squeeze!

But Annis's dreams were
as wild and free as the
forest and moor she
loved so well.

One day, Annis was looking for firewood in the forest when she heard a soft whimpering coming from inside a bramble patch. She peered through the branches and there, looking at her with eyes of summer-sky blue, was a unicorn.

In his foot was a sharp bramble thorn.

Annis's heart swelled with pity. Carefully she prised the thorn from the unicorn's foot. "I will take you back to the castle," she told him. "Grandma has a potion that will heal your foot, and bandages to bind it."

To take the unicorn's mind from the pain, she sang softly to him all the way home.

That night, his foot bandaged and soothed by
the healing potion, the unicorn slept in front
of the fireplace next to Annis and Grandma.
It was a bit of a squeeze! But Annis's dreams
were wild and free – and so were the unicorn's.

The unicorn stayed on in the castle, cared for by
Annis. After a few days, his foot had healed and
he was strong enough for Annis to ride on his
back. Round and round the castle they went, until
eventually they were ready for a real adventure.

That night they galloped over the moors
and through the deep, echoing forest.
Dewdrops sparkled like diamonds on
the ferns and thick branches tangled
overhead. And Annis sang for joy:

> *Over hill and over moor*
>
> *Go Annis and her unicorn.*
>
> *Through the trees, along the stream,*
>
> *The jewelled night is like a dream.*

One moonlit evening, as they rode through the forest, Annis and the unicorn passed a small farm. Nestled in the branches of a nearby tree was a family of fairies, each one no bigger than a baby's hand. Their gossamer wings trembled in the breeze.

Annis gasped with surprise.

"That farm was our home for many years," the fairies
explained, "but the new owners have turned us out. They
will not spare bread and milk for us and our children."

Annis knew she must help. Without a thought, she offered
the fairies shelter in the castle. "The roof leaks, but it's nice
and dry by the great fireplace," she told them. "And
there is milk and bread to spare."

That night it was more of a squeeze than ever in front of the great fireplace.

But while Annis and her grandma, the unicorn, the chickens and the cow slept soundly, the fairies crept away from the hearth and set to work.

All night long
their silver needles
flashed and their
golden hammers
rang out.

And when the sun rose the next morning, a magical
sight awaited Annis and her grandma. The walls of
the castle had been repaired, the roof was mended
and bright curtains hung at every window!

The fairies had also found a chest full of shimmering gowns, which they had washed and darned.
Annis put one on. It was like wearing the softest, sweetest-smelling cloud. "A dress fit for a princess," the fairies declared, and the unicorn nodded in agreement.

That night, thanks to the fairies'
hard work, there was no need for everyone
to sleep squashed in front of the great fireplace.

Grandma moved
into one of the
fine bedrooms.

Annis picked a
chamber with
views of the forest.

The fairies chose
to live in a tower.

The unicorn set up
home in the library.

While the cow settled in the
bathroom with the chickens.

ews of the magnificent castle on the hill, and the beautiful young woman who lived there, spread quickly across the land.

Within days, princes came from far and wide to ask for Annis's hand in marriage. They brought with them costly gifts: bowls of diamonds, bags of gold and boxes of shining silver. Annis had never seen such riches!

The Prince of the North was first to arrive, bearing a chest of brilliant pearls. "Will you marry me, Annis?" he asked.

"I will marry you," said Annis, "if you can answer one question: would you share our castle with the fairy folk?"

"No, fairies cannot be trusted," the prince declared. "They are thieves and cheats."

"In that case," said Annis firmly, "I cannot marry you."

Next came the Prince of the East.
Annis listened to his proposal,
then asked him the same question.
"Would you share our castle
with the fairy folk?"

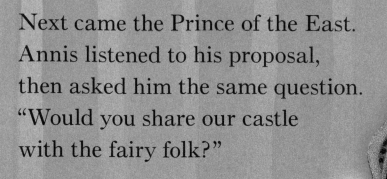

"Certainly not," huffed
the prince. "Fairies are pests –
like mice and rats. What a
nuisance they would be."

"In that case,"
said Annis, "I will
not marry you."

The Prince of the West arrived next. "Fairies bring bad luck," he sniffed when Annis asked her question.

And the Prince of the South just laughed. "Fairies don't exist. What a *ridiculous* idea!"

Annis turned them all away and, each time, the unicorn stamped his hoof and whinnied with delight.

But the unkindness of the princes filled Annis's heart with
sorrow. "If you were a prince," she asked the unicorn,
"would you share your castle with the fairies, and
anyone else who needed a home?"

The unicorn's blue eyes sparkled and
he nodded as if to say yes.

"If only you were a man," sighed Annis,
"then I would marry *you*."

At her words, the unicorn's horn began to glow,
filling the room with dazzling light.

Suddenly, in the unicorn's place, stood a handsome
young man with a golden star on his forehead.

"I *am* a man, Annis – a prince!" he cried.

"Many years ago, a wicked witch put a spell on me.
It could only be broken by the love of a truly kind heart –
like yours. Will you marry me, Annis?" he asked.

Annis laughed for joy. "Yes!" she cried. "And we will
offer a home to the fairies for as long as we live!"

Hundreds of fairies came to help Annis and the Unicorn
Prince celebrate their wedding. The feasting and dancing
lasted all day and all night. Laughter and song rang out over
the hills, and the castle sparkled with the light of a thousand candles.

And from that day on, Annis, her prince, her
grandma, their chickens, their cow and the loyal fairy
folk lived happily in the castle, offering food and shelter
to all those who came knocking – whoever they might be.

And every once in a while, when the moon is
full and the dew sparkles like diamonds on
the heather, Annis's prince turns back into
a unicorn and they go galloping through
the forest and over the magical moors.

Who knows if you might not
meet them one moonlit night?

The
Unicorn
Prince

To Melanie
S.P.

For Clara
and Nyall,
with love.
J.R.

ORCHARD BOOKS

First published in Great Britain in 2018 by The Watts Publishing Group

10 9 8 7 6 5 4 3 2 1

Text © Saviour Pirotta, 2018
Illustrations © Jane Ray, 2018

The moral rights of the author and illustrator have been asserted.

A CIP catalogue record for this book is available from the British Library.

ISBN 978 1 40833 642 7

Printed and bound in China

Orchard Books
An imprint of Hachette Children's Group
Part of The Watts Publishing Group Limited
Carmelite House
50 Victoria Embankment
London EC4Y 0DZ

An Hachette UK Company
www.hachette.co.uk

www.hachettechildrens.co.uk

MIX
Paper from
responsible sources
FSC® C104740
FSC
www.fsc.org